RIDGEVIEW RIDING CLUB

Team Challenge

Bernadette Kelly

Raintree is an imprint of Capstone Global Library Limited,
a company incorporated in England and Wales having its
registered office at 7 Pilgrim Street, London, EC4V 6LB –
Registered company number: 6695582

To contact Raintree, please email myorders@raintreepublishers.co.uk.

First published in Australia by Black Dog Books in 2006
Copyright © Bernadette Kelly 2006
First published in the United Kingdom in 2013
The moral rights of the proprietor have been asserted.

Editor: Laura Knowles
Art Director: Kay Fraser
Graphic Designer: Emily Harris
Production Specialist: Michelle Biedscheid
Originated by Capstone Global Library Ltd
Printed and bound in China

Main cover photograph reproduced with permission
of Shutterstock/© Makarova Viktoria. Background image reproduced
with permission of Shutterstock/© Carlos Caetano.

ISBN 978 1 406 26676 4 (paperback)
17 16 15 14 13
10 9 8 7 6 5 4 3 2 1

British Library Cataloguing in Publication Data
A full catalogue record for this book is available from the British Library.

Team Challenge

Bernadette Kelly

"Why am I doing this?" I asked myself. I was trying to run with both feet in a canvas bag. It was a sack race with a twist – there was a horse involved!

I held my horse's reins with one hand, while I clung to a corner of the bag with the other. For the third time that minute, my feet slipped inside the bag. As I tripped and toppled to the ground in a squirming heap, my grip on the reins loosened. Bobby, my horse, coolly trotted back to the small group of horses and riders standing a short distance away. The other riders seemed pretty amused by my misfortune.

"You're not supposed to let go!" Matt Snyder yelled at me while reaching across to grab Bobby by the bridle.

"That's easy for you to say," I muttered. I kicked my legs free of the bag and jumped to my feet. I wiped a clump of grass, with soil still attached, from the side of my face. Then I scooped up the bag and trudged back to the group. Mr Snyder, our games coach, took the bag from me as I grabbed Bobby's reins.

The reactions from the others in the group only made me angrier. I was sure I could see Jessica Coulson laughing astride her dark show horse, Ripple. I shot her an angry look, which Jessica ignored.

Matt looked frustrated. I thought he and his horse, Bullet, were pretty full of themselves.

Too bad! I thought. *We can't all be great games riders.*

Even Austin Ryan, who wasn't at all interested in mounted games, looked amused by my clumsy attempts to do the sack race. But what upset me the most, what I really hadn't expected, was Reese Moriarty's reaction. Out of everyone from Ridgeview Riding Club, I spent the most time with Reese. I considered her a friend.

Not that we'd always been that way. When I had first moved from the city to Ridgeview, Reese had treated me like I was some dumb city slicker.

Things had begun to change after Bobby, a lovable chestnut horse, was given to me by a local lady, Mrs Cameron. Now, when it came to horses, Reese and I did most things together, along with Bobby and Reese's grey horse, Jefferson.

But here was Reese, openly laughing at my performance in the games lesson.

And Jessica. . .

I turned to Jessica. This was just the kind of behaviour I expected from her.

"It's not funny!" I snapped.

Jessica just widened her eyes, but Reese threw back her head and laughed even harder.

"It's not?" Reese sputtered. "Annie, you should see yourself. You look so funny."

Reese burst into laughter again, then stopped when she saw my hurt expression. "What's the matter?" she asked. "It's only a game, you know, Annie. Don't take it so seriously. Besides, watching you made me remember what I was like when I first tried to run in a sack. Trust me, you're not the only person to struggle with it."

"You can all stop laughing and get serious for a second," Matt interrupted angrily. "Dad will be picking the teams for the regional games day soon. If we want a chance at the county title you'll need to get better. Dad set up practice for next weekend. Everyone has a chance to try out before he chooses the team."

Both Mr Snyder and Matt thought mounted games were the most important part of the riding club, even though there were plenty of other activities: dressage, show jumping, and cross country, for instance.

I thought Matt was lucky to have a father so involved in his son's riding club. My own father didn't seem too interested in what I did with my time – especially my riding time.

Austin couldn't care less about games. He only liked eventing.

"You can count me out," Austin announced. "Cruise isn't built for games, and neither am I.

We'll stick to one-day events." Cruise was Austin's elegant brown thoroughbred mare. Like her owner, she was tall and slim and very athletic.

"Why don't I put you down for assistant team manager, then, Austin?" Mr Snyder offered. "You can help me out with some of the organizing."

A whistle pierced the air. That signalled the end of the lesson. Austin didn't have time to argue. Everyone turned their horses towards the car park, where vehicles and horse trailers were lined up in rows.

Behind the vehicles were holding yards for the horses. We all went our separate ways to unsaddle, feed, and water our horses.

The Ridgeview Riding Club grounds were situated in a large field next to the town's racecourse. There were a couple of buildings. One small shed was used to store equipment.

The other shed contained a small kitchen, with a few tables and chairs.

Reese and I often rode to riding club together. Reese's mother drove her 4×4 over while we rode our horses. She brought along hay, grooming equipment, water buckets, and anything else that might be needed.

Mrs Moriarty was on the parents committee. She usually stayed for the day, preparing and serving lunch in the kitchen.

Reese and I made sure Jefferson and Bobby were unsaddled, brushed down, and happily munching on their hay. Then we made our way across the grounds to the lunch shed.

Once I had a hot dog and a fizzy drink, I glanced around the shed for a seat. Instructors and parents shared a table near the kitchen. The kids mostly sat with other riders from their own groups.

Natalie, Bree, and Sophie, the junior riders, were giggling in the back corner. The seniors had moved outside. Through the wide barn door, I could see Matt's older sister, Laura, and her friends, Hannah and Bryce, sprawled out on the grass. They were deep in conversation.

My group was sitting at the only other table. There was an empty seat between Reese and Matt.

After my humiliation in the games lesson, I wasn't exactly excited to sit there, but I knew it would look weird if I didn't.

The group was still talking about the games team when I sat down. I ate my hot dog while listening to Matt and Reese, who had both ridden at last year's event.

"It's a great event," Reese was saying. "The team has to compete against teams from other clubs. You get points based on how well you do."

Matt added, "And the team with the most points gets to ride in the county finals. Ridgeview has never made it to finals before, let alone won the title."

"Well, no one can say we don't keep trying," Austin said to Matt. "Your dad's been putting a team together every year for as long as I can remember."

"So what games are on the programme?" I asked, after I'd finished off the last bite of my hot dog and gulped down a few mouthfuls of my drink.

Matt answered right away. I could tell that he was obsessed with the topic. "Baton race," he said. "And bottle race, and five-flag race, stepping-stones, rope race . . . oh, and the sack race."

My brain raced to keep up with Matt as he listed the games.

I had never even heard of half of the games. And why did that stupid sack race have to be on the list?

I was interested, even though so far I hadn't really done very well at any of the mounted games. The games day would be a chance to compete for my riding club, as a member of a team.

Then Jessica spoke up. "Well, that leaves Annie out, doesn't it? She's terrible at the sack race and too slow in the other races."

Jessica turned to me and said, "Too bad. The games day sounds kind of cool."

Speechless, I stared at Jessica.

But Matt shook his head. "Anyone from the club can try out for the team," he said.

Instead of feeling thankful to Matt, I felt annoyed.

Yeah, anyone can try out, I thought. *Even useless Annie Boyd.*

"Maybe Annie isn't interested in trying out, Jess," suggested Reese.

Great, I thought. *Another vote of confidence in my skills.*

"Well, I just thought –" began Jessica.

"Since when have you and Ripple been interested in games races, Jess?" I snapped.

Jessica stared at me with a snobby expression. "It's Jess-ica," she announced slowly.

Someone laughed quietly.

"I guess I just haven't been that interested until now," Jessica continued. "I think I should work on Ripple's skills. Of course, that's if there are no shows on that day. Shows are my top priority."

"My top priority is getting to the finals," said Matt. "I want to enter the strongest team possible."

Reese just went on eating her lunch. She wouldn't look at me.

No one thinks I can do it, I thought. *I don't want to be left behind and left out. I'm just going to have to prove them all wrong.*

The next day after school was one of those very rare days when I actually had some free time.

I usually had to stay late at school to wait for my mother, who was a teacher there. Another thing that took up a lot of my time was my job at a local stable. My boss, Erica, who was also the dressage instructor at the riding club, usually needed me to work several hours a week.

Erica expected me to work hard for her and do everything perfectly, but she was also willing to offer advice when I needed it. Thanks to Erica, I had learned a lot about riding and caring for horses.

When I had overheard Reese at school discussing extra practice, I'd offered to join her. But then I worried that I wasn't welcome. I suspected that Reese thought it was a waste of time for me to practice, since I wouldn't be good enough to make the team anyway. I decided to try to prove Reese wrong.

I had to admit, though, that Reese had been nice about the whole practice thing. "Just tell your mum you're coming home with me," she had said. "Then you can go next door and get changed before we start."

So, that day after school, we were in Reese's barn, looking for things to use for games equipment.

We were planning to get in an unofficial practice at home before Mr Snyder's practice. All I could see of my friend was a pair of pale blue jodhpurs, with dusty riding boots on her feet. Her entire upper body was buried inside a steel drum.

Reese popped out, holding a couple of old feedbags. "Found 'em. Here's our sacks," she said.

Reese pointed in the direction of the door. "There's a recycling bin in the corner, over there," she told me. "Grab two empty bottles. We'll rinse them out and use them for the bottle race."

I looked for the bin. Inside was a jumbled pile of empty plastic juice bottles, milk cartons, and soft drink cans. I fished among the empty containers and dragged out two clear plastic bottles. I held them up for Reese to see.

"Are these the ones?" I asked.

When Reese nodded, I took the bottles outside. Reese walked out from the shed. The feedbags were over her shoulder. She was also carrying a bunch of skipping ropes.

"I found a few skipping ropes," Reese told me happily. "I remember playing with them when I was little."

I reached out and took the ropes from her. "I don't have any of my old toys left," I said. "Mum threw them all out or gave them away before we moved."

"Oh, that's sad!" Reese said. "I would hate to lose all my old stuff." Then she added, "We can use these for the rope race." She scanned the back garden, looking thoughtful.

Then I noticed a broom propped against the wall of Reese's house. "Can we use that for something?" I asked, pointing over at the broom.

"Perfect!" said Reese. "We can use it for the five-flag race. Do you have any old oil drums at Hillgrove?"

Hillgrove was the name of my family's farm. I frowned and pictured the inside of our barn. I thought I could remember a couple of old drums that had been left behind by the previous owners. My dad had mentioned throwing them out, but I didn't think he'd done it yet.

"I think there might be two," I said hesitantly.

"Great," said Reese. "Let's go. We can practice at your place."

After the hot day, the air outside was finally beginning to cool down. Reese and I threw all the games equipment over the fence and then scrambled between the wires. We stuffed the bottles and jump ropes into the feedbags.

Reese took the broom in one hand and dragged a bag with the other, while I carried the second bag. My dog, a little terrier named Jonesy, came running to meet us. He yapped out one sharp bark to say hello. Then he trotted happily beside me.

We dumped the equipment at the gate to Bobby's corral, which the horse shared with my father's six sheep. I knew that my father thought the sheep were really special and way more useful than my horse.

Bobby and his woolly companions grazed peacefully together most of the time. But sometimes, when Bobby was feeling playful, he would chase them into a tight little group of six, then run them around and around the fence line until he got bored of the game and went back to eating grass.

Reese returned home to saddle up Jefferson while I searched for more equipment. I found the two old drums exactly where I had thought they would be. I tipped them onto their sides and rolled them to the gate. Then I half-filled the bottles with dirt from a corner of my father's vegetable garden.

My dad was very proud of his homegrown vegetables. In our old city apartment, there hadn't been room for a garden. Soon after our family moved here, he staked out a site, turned the soil over, and bought some seedlings.

Now he took care of his garden every day when he got home from work. He spent weekends weeding and harvesting. He loved to say to visitors, "Check out these tomatoes!"

I had to admit that the vegetables looked impressive. I knew my father had used Bobby's manure to enrich the soil before he'd planted his precious crops, including the tomato plants that were neatly spaced and carefully staked along the back row.

So there you go, Dad, I thought, grinning. *Bobby is good for something after all.*

I hurried to saddle up and meet up with Reese for our practice session.

The practice session had some unexpected results.

After Reese returned with Jefferson, she had me hold him. She rolled out the drums and spaced them in a line about thirty yards apart. Then she set one soil-filled bottle on top of the farthest drum.

The sheep ran off to a corner as far away from them as possible. Then they stood, staring nervously.

Jonesy sat near the gate watching what we were doing. His mouth hung open in a happy grin. His watchful eyes didn't miss a single moment.

"We'll start with the bottle race," Reese said. "The games are all relays. The teams line up behind the starting line. For the bottle race, the first rider leaves the start holding a bottle. At the first drum, the rider places the bottle on the top, then rides to the next drum, picks up a different bottle and returns to the start to hand that bottle to the next rider, who takes the bottle to the second drum, drops it on the top of that drum, and then picks up the bottle from the first drum on the way back. Each rider has to place a bottle on the empty drum and collect a bottle from the other drum. Are you following this?" Reese asked me. I nodded.

"Okay." Reese picked up the other bottle and mounted Jefferson. "I'll start."

Reese waved at an imaginary starting line on the ground. Holding the bottle and riding one-handed, Reese urged Jefferson into a canter. They thundered away.

I couldn't help but be impressed as I watched Reese lean over Jefferson's side, still cantering, and smoothly deposit the bottle on the drum before flying off to pick up the second bottle and return to the start.

Reese held out the bottle as she approached me, waiting for me to take it from her. But I was so busy admiring Reese that I forgot my own part in the game. I sat on Bobby's back with both hands loose at my sides. Reese's irritated expression as she passed with the bottle shook me out of my daydream. But, of course, it was too late. Reese brought Jefferson to a stop.

"Are we practicing, or not?" Reese sputtered furiously.

"Sorry. It's just . . . wow, Reese," I said. "You're as good at this as Matt is!"

"Don't tell Matt that," Reese said, but she sounded happy. "Can we try again? And this time, pay attention!"

Reese repeated the routine. I kept my eye on the bottle and stretched out my arm as Jefferson thundered towards me.

Everything was going fine until the moment I closed my hand around the bottle and nudged Bobby forwards with my legs. The soil shook up and down inside the bottle.

As we crossed the starting line, I was focused on the drum and thinking about the way I would bend down to place the bottle on top. But Bobby didn't like the noise made by the soil shaking up and down inside the plastic. Eyeing the bottle as if it were something scary, Bobby moved sharply away.

I was jolted sideways. My left foot slipped from the stirrup. Desperately, I tried to cling to the saddle, while still holding the reins and the bottle. I felt the bottle slipping from my hand at the same time as my body began to tip to the right.

The next thing I heard was a loud pop. The plastic bottle split its sides when I landed on it. Most of the dirt ended up smeared all over my jodhpurs. Unhurt, but red-faced, I rose to my feet and dusted myself off.

"Are you okay?" Reese asked.

I nodded. "It was the bottle. Bobby –"

"Yeah, I know," said Reese. "It's so weird, the things that horses worry about. We have to desensitize him to it."

I slipped my foot back into the stirrup and swung myself into the saddle.

"Do what?" I asked.

Reese turned Jefferson and rode back to get the other bottle from the top of the drum. Holding the reins in one hand and the bottle in the other, she casually cantered back to me. I was jealous of Reese's easy riding style.

"Desensitize him," she repeated, then dismounted. "You get off, too," Reese ordered.

I just got back on, I thought, feeling annoyed, but I dismounted anyway. Once I had both feet on the ground, Reese held up the bottle and shook it firmly. I almost lost my hold on the reins as Bobby startled and flung his head back and away from the offending sound.

"Whoa!" I tried to soothe Bobby before I snapped at Reese, "What did you do that for?"

Reese's response was to shake the bottle again. Bobby's head went up and he eyed the bottle nervously, but his reaction was far less violent than before.

"See? He's getting used to it," said Reese, shaking the bottle again. "He's only afraid of the noise because it's something new."

This time Bobby hardly spooked at all. Reese and I remounted and positioned ourselves behind the start line. We ran through the whole routine again. Success! I caught Reese's pass and managed to deposit and pick up the bottles in the right places.

"We'll try the sack race now," Reese announced after we had practiced the bottle routine half a dozen times.

I groaned. "Ugh! I'm terrible at that one." Then I brightened as I had an idea. "Maybe, if I'm picked for the team, I can just skip the sack race!"

But Reese was shaking her head even before the words were fully out of my mouth. "Don't count on that happening. You'll have to ride whatever races Mr Snyder puts you in."

I still wasn't feeling confident with the games day events, but my worst fear was the sack race. I was still covered in bruises from the last time.

It might only be practice, but it still hurts when you fall over, I thought nervously.

Not that it mattered anyway. I remembered how good Reese had been at the bottle race. If all the others at Ridgeview rode games as well as she did, I didn't have a chance of being picked for the team.

"Push your feet hard into the corners and hold the bag as high around your middle as you can," Reese told me seriously. "That's the secret to not falling over." Reese rode to an imaginary point at the end of the line. She dropped the bag and cantered back to the start.

"You go first," said Reese, "I'll start you." I waited. Then Reese lifted her arm and shouted, "Go!"

Bobby and I trotted away to where the bag lay on the ground. I wanted to urge Bobby into a canter, but I was worried I might have trouble stopping him at the bag.

I remembered what Jessica had said. "Annie's terrible at the sack race and too slow in the other races."

I'll take it slow and steady the first time, I told myself. I dismounted and pulled the bag over my legs. I was so busy with the bag that I hardly noticed my fingers slipping from the reins. I wasn't holding him, but Bobby just stood quietly beside me.

Finally, I was in the bag. I clutched it to me and was about to begin the long jump back to Reese. Then my friend rode up to me, scowling.

"You can't let go!" she yelled at me. "In a real competition you would have gotten the whole team disqualified!"

I stared at her. "Let go of what? What did I do?"

"You let go of the reins," Reese told me. "The rules say that you must keep one hand on the reins at all times."

Guiltily, I snatched at Bobby's reins with one hand, leaving one side of the bag to slip down my side.

"What's with you?" I asked. "I thought you said this was only a game!"

Reese smiled an apology. "Sorry. It's just that it would be so great to see Ridgeview finally win and get to the county championship."

I had known that Matt was obsessed with the coming competition, but I was starting to think that Reese was even more obsessed.

I sighed and frowned sadly at Reese. "This is hopeless," I said quietly. "I can't do anything right. Maybe I shouldn't even try out for the team. The last thing I want is to get the team disqualified."

My friend's silence left me feeling worse. Obviously, Reese had doubts about my riding abilities, too.

Reese turned to the starting line. "Come on. Let's try again. Just start from there."

I pulled the sack up around my waist again and began to jump. Reese's advice about pushing my toes into the bag really helped, although I still managed to trip twice on the way back to Reese.

Reese took another turn, then handed the bag to me again. This time, I held the bag in one hand and the reins in the other, and actually managed a canter on the way down the line.

As I dismounted, I ignored the one sheep that had gotten away from the rest of the pack and was grazing near the imaginary competition field. Once in the bag, I began to shuffle my way back.

Right then, Jonesy spotted the wandering sheep and took off after it.

The startled sheep, with the dog in pursuit, cut straight across my path. Too late, Reese yelled, "Look out!" The sheep, dog, horse, and I collided in a tangled pile.

Instantly, Bobby pulled away. That left me on top of the stunned sheep, with Jonesy on top of me.

At that very moment, my father arrived home. I groaned as I heard his car drive up. I wasn't hurt, but I didn't want to know what my dad would say when he saw his daughter tangled in a feedbag and lying on one of his precious sheep.

The sheep gave one loud scared bleat before struggling to its feet and running away. I tried to get up, but halfway up I tripped on the bag and flopped back to the ground.

So much for the sack race, I thought.

"Annie!"

I winced. I was sure my father's angry yell could be heard all the way to the main street of Ridgeview. I caught Reese's eye as my father slammed his car door closed and marched towards me.

Reese mouthed the words, "I'll call you later," before quickly riding away through the gate behind my dad.

I didn't blame her. I would have left, too, if I could.

"Just what on earth do you think you're doing?" my father roared at me. "You cannot be bothering my sheep. This is totally unacceptable, Annie."

"The sheep got in the way," I tried to explain. "We were practicing for the –"

"I don't care what you were doing," my father said angrily. "You leave those sheep alone." He shook his head, and then added, "I don't know, Annie. Since you got that horse, you're just not thinking. You're not the same, and I think it's the horse's fault."

I drew in my breath sharply. My father could be so annoying. He hadn't wanted Bobby in the first place. Now, he used any chance he had to complain about my horse.

My father looked around at the games equipment in the pasture. "And get rid of all this junk," he ordered.

He never listened to me. And I was sick of him always blaming Bobby. It wasn't Bobby's fault, and I hadn't done anything wrong.

My father waved a finger at me. "It's about time you considered the rest of us around here, and not just that horse!"

I was the one who took care of the horse. I did everything. I fed him, cared for him, and made sure he was healthy.

My dad didn't do a thing. So why did he make such a fuss? I couldn't understand it.

And it wasn't like I ignored my family. I was polite. I showed up for all of the meals. I tried to talk to my parents about my interests. He was the one who ignored me!

Dad walked away, leaving me staring angrily at his back.

Reese and I rode together to the riding club grounds for Mr Snyder's practice session.

We trotted past several small farm properties before taking a rough dirt path leading into the national forest. We slowed the horses to a walk as trees closed in around us, thrusting us into shadow.

The only sounds that morning were the rustle of birds in the trees and the soft, regular thump of the horses' feet as they moved along in a four-beat rhythm.

I broke the silence. I wanted to talk to Reese about my dad's outburst.

"I'm sorry about the other day," I said awkwardly. "My dad . . . he doesn't have much patience for horses."

"It's fine," said Reese. She hesitated a moment. Then, with a sigh, she added, "At least he's not pushing you to win everything all the time."

I turned to Reese with surprise. "What do you mean?" I asked.

Reese looked down at her saddle. Her answer was muffled. "You'll see," she said. "Just wait until the games day."

At the riding club grounds, the equipment needed for each game had been brought out of the shed and set up for the practice. People talked about the coming competition. The whole morning would be used for practicing.

Then the teams would finally be chosen after lunch.

Mr Snyder wasted no time getting started. First, he explained how things were done. I learned that there were rules about riders making mistakes.

If someone dropped the handover to the next rider, that rider would have to dismount, pick up the stick or baton, and hand it to the new rider. The pass had to be made between the start line and the six-yard line.

Anything knocked over during the race had to be righted by the offending rider, before they could complete the run and the next rider could take their turn to race.

"But don't worry too much if you do make a mistake," Mr Snyder told us. "Just fix it and keep going. It's better to slow down a little and do it right than to go too fast and mess it up."

I watched the others, especially Matt and his sister Laura. There wasn't a race that the two of them weren't experts at. I mentioned it to Reese.

"The Snyder family has a long history of games competitions," said Reese. "Matt and Laura have been riding in mounted games since before they could even walk."

"They've got a great teacher," I said. "Their dad is always so calm and encouraging. I'd hate to be teaching this to newcomers like me, but Mr Snyder never seems to get annoyed or frustrated."

I couldn't ride as fast as Matt and Laura, so I took Mr Snyder's advice and tried for accuracy instead of speed.

I liked the five-flag race. I didn't think I was too bad at putting a flag into the drum, rounding the barrel, and then snatching up another flag on the way back to the line.

The stepping-stone dash involved dismounting, stepping along a row of blocks, and then remounting in a race to the finish line. I noticed that the fastest riders were the ones who could dismount and then vault back on without stopping the horse – something neither Jessica nor I could do.

Austin's little sister, Natalie, was really fast. Her small pony gave her an advantage. In the bottle race, she didn't even have to bend to pick up the bottle.

In the bending race, the only thing I had to do was zigzag through a line of poles. I loved the swaying feeling as Bobby's cantering body curved left and right between the poles. This turned out to be my best race.

The sack race was still a problem. I couldn't seem to do it. I just hoped it wouldn't affect my chances when it was time for the teams to be chosen.

When the team was being announced, Mr Snyder called out the names one by one. He seemed tense. Matt and Laura were chosen first, which surprised nobody.

Next came Natalie. She looked pleased to have been chosen for the team.

I looked across to Austin, who leaned against a fence, watching the proceedings. He wasn't concerned with riding in the team himself, but he seemed really happy when his sister was chosen.

Reese smiled happily when she was picked. I felt a small thrill for her. She deserved the place after all her effort and practice.

Next, Bryce, from Laura's group, had his name called. I had heard Austin telling Matt that Georgie and Hannah, the two other seniors, weren't interested in being part of the team as both of them would be away on the games day.

My heart lurched. Five riders had been chosen, but six were needed to make a team. Did I still have a chance?

Mr Snyder fell silent for a moment. He cleared his throat a couple of times and shifted his weight from one foot to the other.

"There is one place left," he announced to the waiting group. "At this point we are undecided between two riders."

I glanced around. The only people left were Bree, Sophie, Jessica, and me.

I knew I still had to do a better job at the games, but so did Jessica, and the younger girls had also been slow.

Mr Snyder continued, "We've decided to have two substitutes. Both riders will practice with the team. The actual team rider will be announced a few days before the games day." Barely breathing, I waited.

"The substitutes are Jessica Coulson and Annie Boyd," Mr Snyder announced.

I realized I'd been holding my breath. I let out the stale air and took a deep breath. Jessica was staring at me. I stared back.

Mr Snyder's decision gave me hope. I wasn't out of it yet. I really wanted a place on the team. Why did I have to compete against Jessica to get it?

Chapter Six

Mr Snyder seemed determined to have the best team in the county. He wanted to win. He insisted that the team meet after school every night for practice. I knew I couldn't miss a single practice. What if that made him choose Jessica instead of me?

I begged Erica, my boss, to let me take some time off from the stables.

Erica, with an amused look in her eye, acted as if she thought the whole team was completely crazy to be taking it all so seriously.

"It's only games," she told me. "If you were practicing for a major dressage competition, I'd give you a whole week off with pay!"

Despite Erica's teasing, she agreed to let me off the hook until after the games day.

I had noticed that Matt never stopped his horse to get on and off while riding in the games. Instead, he leaped onto Bullet's back while the horse was still moving. I wondered if I could learn to do that. A skill like that would help me when it came to being picked for the team.

I went to the school library to search for information about mounted games. There wasn't much, only historical stuff about mounted war games. I didn't think that riders were going to be stabbing each other with jousting sticks or sword fighting on horseback at the regional games day. Still, I checked out some of the websites.

I found a page on vaulting. That's what Matt's little trick was called. I read that vaulting was another skill that had originated in wartime. When soldiers needed to make a quick escape, they would run beside their horses, leap on, and gallop away.

"So how did Matt learn to vault?" I asked Reese the next day.

Reese laughed. "He makes it look easy," she said. "But it takes a lot of experience. I've managed to do it a couple of times, but I don't try it when I'm in a race. If you screw it up, it wastes more time than it saves."

I watched Matt carefully whenever I could. At home, I tried vaulting onto the fence. The first time I ran up to the fence and leapt, reaching for the bottom rail with my foot. Although I managed to throw my leg over the fence, the landing was hard, and I almost rolled right off again.

I decided to try the real version. I ran alongside Bobby while he was trotting. To keep him going, I had to pull him along with the bridle. To vault, I needed to turn and face Bobby's side. The second I stopped pulling the horse along, he would stop. This left me jumping up from a standstill.

Even then, I couldn't do it. I would use all my strength and leap. But I couldn't even get my foot across Bobby's back, let alone find enough spring in my legs to swing into the saddle from ground level.

The team, however, was improving with all the practice. I was learning to lean over my horse and snatch up the bottle in my hand without slowing.

Bobby wasn't afraid of the rattling noise anymore. My other skills were improving, too, like grabbing flags as I passed the drums, and passing the baton without dropping it.

Matt was always pushing everyone to go faster. "We have to be the fastest," he would yell as he and Bullet raced back over the line one more time. I lost count of how many times they ran through each race.

Mr Snyder, too, wanted the team to be the best we could be. Mostly, he was interested in the team becoming more accurate – making fewer mistakes in each game – even if that meant we had to slow down a bit.

"Remember the old saying," he would say when someone tried to go too fast and dropped a baton or missed a flag. "Slow and steady wins the race."

Jessica had improved, too. I kept an uneasy eye on her progress. By the glances I'd seen being thrown my way, I knew Jessica was doing the same.

As far as I could tell, we were running about equal in the competition for the last place on the team. From what I'd seen, I didn't think Jessica had improved any more than I had.

I did have one concern, however. In the sack race, Jessica was really great, and I was still terrible. She could tuck her feet into the bag and do a kind of skip to the line. She was pretty fast and hardly ever fell, while I hadn't been able to complete even one race without ending up on the ground.

I had to wait until the next riding club rally day to find out whether or not I was part of the official games team.

The night before, I dreamt that Jessica and I were racing each other, but our horses were harnessed to carriages and we were both wearing fancy silk racing clothes. We were neck and neck. Then, out of nowhere, my horse suddenly dropped his head and began to graze. I had to get out of the carriage and drag Bobby along by the bridle.

Jessica and Ripple passed the line, cheered on by a crowd of supporters. There at the finish line was a smiling show judge, waiting to pin a ribbon on Ripple and shake Jessica's hand.

As I struggled to get my horse across the line, the crowd turned ugly. Boos and hisses rang in my ears.

I woke up early. My pillow was on the floor, and the sheets were all tangled up by my feet.

And it was only going to get worse.

I had trouble with my riding club tie when I got dressed in my uniform for the rally. Finally, I gave up and asked my father to help, which meant putting up with a lecture about learning to do things for myself. The toaster was broken. It burned my bread black as a horse's hoof and just as tough. And then, when I went to Bobby's paddock, he refused to let me catch him.

By the time I had followed the horse around the paddock for twenty minutes, I was ready to catch one of the sheep and ride it to the riding club instead. It didn't help my bad mood when Reese arrived and walked straight up to Bobby, slipping the halter over his nose as casually as if he were her own.

Finally, and more than a little late, we were tacked up and on our way.

That morning was devoted to practice. We practiced passing, mounting, and dismounting. Then we ran mock races. I was really proud of the new skills I was learning.

When it came to my riding, whenever I learned something new, I felt a deep sense of pride, satisfaction, and happiness. The long and sometimes painful process of learning to ride had been worth it. I loved the partnership I had formed with Bobby.

Finally, after lunch, the time had come for Mr Snyder to make his announcement. The room fell silent as the games instructor cleared his throat. I stood perfectly still, waiting for the announcement.

"The final member of our games team is. . ." He paused, and I took a deep breath and closed my eyes.

Finally, Mr Snyder said, "Jessica Coulson, with Annie Boyd as our substitute."

For a moment, I was stunned. I had worked so hard. But he had chosen Jessica.

My eyes filled with tears. I quickly turned away, but not before seeing Jessica turn to me and raise her eyebrows.

I reached up to touch my face. It was hot. Suddenly, my tie was too tight. I needed air. I pretended not to notice Reese and Matt looking at each other over my head.

In my hurry to leave the shed, I crashed into a chair, knocking it over. I stepped over it. Then I stumbled outside. The air inside the shed was thick with the smell of hot dogs and hamburgers from the grill. It was making me feel sick.

So, that's it then, I thought. *I'm not on the team. I'm not good enough. How could I have ever thought I would be?*

I made my way to Bobby. He had finished his hay and was standing with his eyes closed, dozing. At the sound of my footsteps, he opened his eyes and nickered softly.

I entered the yard and leaned against Bobby's side. I buried my head in his mane and quietly began to sob. Bobby nuzzled at my arm. He was looking for an apple, his favourite treat.

I pulled back and looked into the horse's eyes. Wet tears blurred my sight. "It's just one day," I told the horse. "What do I care? They're just dumb games anyway."

"They're not dumb. But I'd be disappointed, too, if I were you," a boy's voice said. "But you're still the substitute, so you get to come on the day. You may get to ride after all. It's happened before, you know."

Embarrassed, I swung around. Matt was standing at the fence. I wiped my eyes hurriedly.

The tail of Matt's white shirt hung over his jodhpurs. A dark green grass stain was smeared over the bottom half of his sleeve.

He saw me looking at it. "Bullet likes to rub slobber on me when I take his bridle off," he said. "Mum always says I don't have any white shirts, only green and white ones."

Even with my current troubles, I smiled. Matt was always the messy one at the riding club. His looks seemed to be a long way down on his list of what was important.

"I just hoped. . ." I began, then shook my head. "It doesn't matter. I'm not really very good at games, anyway."

"No, that's not true," said Matt. "You're as good as Jessica is. But there was only one spot, and my dad had to make a choice."

I nodded. I knew Matt was right. But that didn't make me feel any better. I thought about Jessica. If I was honest with myself, I knew that what hurt the most was that it was Jessica who beat me.

"It was the sack race, wasn't it?" I asked quietly.

Matt's cheeks reddened slightly, but he stayed silent.

"I saw the look on her face," I went on. "Why does she hate me so much?"

Matt stepped up onto the bottom rail of the yard and leaned over.

"Jessica's a spoiled brat," he said. Then he grinned. "Besides, she's rude to everyone, so don't think you're special."

Just then, Reese appeared and Matt left to saddle up for the afternoon sessions.

Before we remounted, Reese threw her arm around me and gave me a hug. "It's not such a big deal to make the team, you know," she said, smiling at me. "And there's always next year."

"You can help me manage the team," Austin said when he saw me in the jumping lesson.

Jessica acted the same as she always did and ignored me, which was fine because I didn't think I wanted to deal with having a fight with her.

After the rally was over, Mr Snyder took me aside to explain my job as the substitute. "Sometimes a rider gets sick or a horse gets hurt," he told me. "That's where you would step in and take over. We'll need you to come on the day, with your horse, and stand by just in case."

Just in case, I thought bitterly that night at home. *Instead of being a real team member, I'm the just-in-case girl.*

I had really wanted to ask Mr Snyder why. Why had Jessica been chosen and not me? But I didn't ask.

I hadn't wanted to seem rude by questioning the coach's decision. I wanted to forget all about the games day, but I would be letting the team down if I did that. Everyone, except Jessica of course, was being so nice to me. It wasn't their fault I was stuck being the substitute rider.

I had a feeling that Jessica would probably rub in her victory whenever she could. The bad dream I had the night before now felt like it was coming true.

Then Reese's mother called, and things got even worse.

"That would be wonderful, Clara," said my mum. "Yes, of course we'll be happy to have Reese with us. I know the O'Briens won't mind at all. We'll make a weekend of it. The O'Briens? They have two kids – Dave and Jade. Jade and Annie have been friends for years. I'm sure the girls will have a fabulous time."

Mum hung up the phone and turned to me. "Clara has offered to take both the horses to the games day next weekend," she told me. "We can stay overnight at the O'Briens' house in the city and meet Clara the next day. What do you think? Won't that be fun?"

Now I had something else to worry about.

The games day was being held at a riding school several hours away, on the other side of the county. Mum had arranged for Reese's mother to take the horses.

The rest of us would be breaking up the trip by staying overnight at Jade's house.

Ever since Jade O'Brien had rescued me from Gina Toppolino, who was a year older and twice my size, Jade and I had been best friends.

Gina had tried to bully me into handing over my lunch money while we waited in line for lunch one day in Year Three. Just as I was about to give up, Jade had "accidentally" stood on Gina's foot. Then she drew everyone's attention to Gina by making a big show of apologizing. Gina had been forced to buy lunch with her own money that day. And she never picked on me again.

Now that I had moved away, Jade and

I hardly saw each other, but we still kept in touch by phone and email. I told Jade about my experiences with Bobby, and Jade kept me up to date with the gossip from my old school.

Jade was a city kid, into shopping and girl stuff. But Reese didn't seem to care about anything except horses and riding. Would the two of them get along? I really wasn't sure.

Chapter Eight

My family followed Mrs Moriarty's 4×4 and horse trailer all the way from Ridgeview. This was the first time that I had been back to the city since my family moved.

It had been early that morning when we had left the peace of Hillgrove, with its shady trees and open fields, and hit the road.

My father, an estate agent, liked to talk about every single property we passed. I thought it was incredibly boring.

Reese and I soon started up our own conversation in the back seat, blocking out the talk of the adults.

"Are you nervous about tomorrow?" I asked Reese.

"Kind of," Reese replied. "But I'm more excited than anything. Games competitions are always really fun."

I fell silent. I had almost, but not quite, come to terms with the fact that I wasn't really a part of the team. As far as I knew, no person or horse from the Ridgeview team had become sick or injured. Since the games day was in less than 24 hours, I was pretty sure no one would.

The day was going to be fun – everyone said so. But I wasn't sure what would be fun about watching the others racing while I just stood on the sidelines. In fact, I was pretty sure it wouldn't be fun at all.

Soon, it was time to part from Mrs Moriarty and the horses. We waved goodbye as our car took a left turn towards the city, and Mrs Moriarty's 4×4 continued on down the motorway.

I felt weird watching my horse being driven away, even though I knew I'd see him again tomorrow. I hoped Mrs Moriarty would take care of him as well as I would have.

Because the horses would be gone overnight, we had mixed up two feeds for each horse. The feeds were made up of chaff and barley with molasses added. Reese and I had cut up some apples and thrown the pieces in before pouring the feeds into individual bags. Then we sealed them and stowed the bags in Mrs Moriarty's horse trailer.

It was already late morning. I stared out of the car window at row after row of houses and grey, hard concrete. Not so long ago, this had been where I lived and went to school, where my friends and entertainment were. This place had been my home.

Now everything looked the same, but it felt different. The closed spaces and concrete surfaces made me feel as if I was driving through a tunnel. It was nothing like the open roads around Ridgeview.

Finally the car stopped. We all piled out and dragged the overnight bags from the trunk. A teenager was washing a car in the driveway. He raised his hand and waved at us.

"Hey, Dave," I called out. "That's Jade's brother," I told Reese.

Mrs O'Brien answered the door with a welcoming grin. "Hi, Annie!" she said, giving me a quick hug. "Jade will be so excited to see you. She hasn't stopped talking about this for days."

Jade squealed when she saw me. We rushed to hug each other. Then I pointed to Reese, who stood outside the door, watching us.

"Jade, this is Reese," I said. "She's my new next-door neighbour and my riding buddy."

"Hello." Jade's greeting was quiet. She looked Reese up and down.

Reese wore jeans and a baggy T-shirt with a cartoon horse head on the front. On her feet were a pair of old, ratty trainers. They had once been white but now they were tinged with dusty brown from spending so much time outside.

It occurred to me that Reese's outfit, although perfect weekend wear for Ridgeview, was totally out of place here. I should have warned Reese before we left. I sighed. Hopefully Reese wouldn't mind that she wasn't dressed right.

I had found one of my old outfits from when we still lived in the city. Wearing a short, faded denim skirt and brightly coloured, tightly fitting top, I knew I would fit in.

Even though I knew I was dressed right for the city, I checked out Jade's outfit. She looked great. She was wearing a cute white beaded top with spaghetti straps and a pale blue ruffled skirt. On her feet was a pair of beaded white sandals.

Reese didn't say anything to Jade. She just nodded. She didn't look very happy.

I stared from one to the other nervously. What was wrong with them?

I had already decided that this time at Jade's house was probably the only fun I was going to have for the weekend. But that wasn't going to happen if my two friends didn't like each other.

"So, Jade," I said, breaking the silence. "We've got all afternoon and evening. What should we do?"

Mrs O'Brien turned to us. "Why don't you three girls head down to the shopping centre for a while?" she suggested. "You could get some lunch while you're there and maybe pick out a film to watch this evening. Your mum and dad are coming out for dinner with us, Annie. You kids can stay home and order a pizza. How does that sound?"

Jade shrugged.

Reese had made no move to enter the house. She was staring at the O'Brien's light blue carpet. I guessed it was her dusty shoes that were making her worried. She didn't want to step on the carpet and leave a dirty footprint.

"Sounds like a plan," I said quickly. "Well, I can't wait! Let's go."

I grabbed Jade's arm and waved at Reese to follow.

Jade and Reese just need some time to get to know each other, I thought.

By the time we had all spent a couple of hours together, Jade and Reese would be sure to click. The three of us would have a fantastic night together.

The shopping centre was just like I remembered. It was built on three levels and the shops were grouped around the edges of the building, with a wide courtyard and escalators in the middle.

We headed straight for the food court. I walked into Tony's Restaurant. The small café was full of chrome and white tables and chairs. I was searching for a particular table, where Jade and I had always shared our favourite snack.

The best thing on the menu at Tony's was nachos. The tortilla chips were topped with thick layers of melted cheese, spicy peppers, chopped tomatoes, and diced onions. They were finished with a fist-sized blob of sour cream and another of guacamole.

Jade and I had always ordered the nachos whenever we came to Tony's. We would also have big, steaming mugs of hot chocolate.

Tony's was the place where we had come whenever we went to the shopping centre, which had been often. Sometimes we went every day after school. We would sit at our favourite table and discuss the latest film or compare purchases from our shopping trip.

A family had the nerve to be sitting at "our" table. Disappointed, I chose another booth and flopped into a chair.

Reese and Jade both sat down.

Reese picked up the menu. "What should I get to eat?" she asked.

"We always get nachos and hot chocolate," Jade told her.

Reese continued to scan the menu. She said, "I hate nachos. I'm getting pizza."

Jade frowned. "But Annie and I always have nachos!" she said.

Reese looked annoyed. She turned towards Jade. Before she could speak, I said, "It doesn't matter, Jade. That's our tradition, not Reese's. Why don't we have something else for a change? We can all have pizza."

Jade shot me a disgusted look. Then she said, "You two go right ahead. I'm having nachos. Like I always do, when I come here with my friends."

Reese got a lemonade, and she and I split a medium pizza. I wanted to make Jade happy, so I ordered a hot chocolate, even though it wasn't going to taste right with the pizza.

"We should go over to Movie Masters after this," Jade said once we had ordered our food. She ignored Reese and spoke directly to me. "I want to get the DVD of *Glitter Girl*. It's supposed to be really good," she said. "I saw the previews but I didn't get a chance to see it when it was on at the cinema because I was too busy. It's about this girl who becomes a fashion model when –"

"A fashion model?" Reese snorted impatiently. "Who in their right mind would want to watch a film about a fashion model? Some ditzy teenager who walks around being a moving coat hanger!"

An angry, dark look suddenly crossed Jade's face. I winced. Reese had just totally trashed Jade's dream in life, which was to be a fashion model.

"Yeah, well, maybe you should watch it and pick up a few tips about how to dress," Jade snapped back.

"There's nothing wrong with my outfit." Reese didn't care. "At least I'm not following the rest of the sheep."

I sighed. Right now, being a sheep sounded like a better choice than sitting between my two best friends, who both seemed determined to hate each other.

Chapter Ten

From Jade's front doorstep, Jade and I waved goodbye to our parents. Mrs O'Brien handed Jade a slip of paper as she left.

"Your brother is going out tonight, so I wrote down all our mobile numbers for you," she told her daughter. "Call us right away in an emergency. We'll be at Orlando's Restaurant."

"We'll be fine, Mum," Jade said, rolling her eyes. "There's plenty of food, and we're going to watch a DVD."

While Jade ushered her mother out the door, Reese sat in the living room. She was clutching her throat and pretending to gag when Jade mentioned the film.

I was annoyed with both of them. Instead of the fun time I had expected to have in the city, I had spent an uncomfortable afternoon trying to not make anyone angry. Meanwhile, both of my friends, the new and the old, did their best to ignore each other.

Jade had got her own way. We'd rented *Glitter Girl*, much to Reese's disgust. Well, I'd had enough of them both. Reese could have kept her mouth shut. We were guests in Jade's house, after all.

And Jade! Why did she have to keep making fun of Reese's clothes? It wasn't a crime to have your own style, was it?

The weekend was turning from bad to worse. I had been disappointed enough about my substitute place on the games team. Now I was stuck in a house with two people who refused to speak to each other.

In the living room, Reese picked up the remote control. She turned on the television and began flicking through the channels. Jade was clattering dishes in the kitchen.

I glanced at Reese, but she didn't look at me. So I gave up and headed into the kitchen to help Jade. We moved from one room to the other, laying out a selection of snacks on the O'Brien's coffee table.

Jade had found an oversized bowl and filled it with crisps. Then she opened a box of savoury crackers, added a couple of dips, and finally a can of cola for each of us.

As I moved in and out of the living room, I caught glimpses of the TV screen. Faded black and grey war footage flashed up, followed by a game show.

Reese finally settled on a programme featuring music videos.

She gave an excited gasp when a cute, curly-haired guy with a guitar on his lap appeared on the TV.

"Hey, Annie," she called. "It's Joel Flanagan. He's so cool."

I did a double take and almost dropped the three cans I had tucked in my arms.

I had heard of Joel Flanagan. Who hadn't? But I had no idea that Reese liked him. I had never even heard Reese mention music. All we had ever talked about were horses.

Suddenly, Jade came running in from the kitchen.

"This is his new song," Jade announced. "I read about it in *Who Knows Who*. He wrote it when he broke up with his girlfriend. So sad! I couldn't believe it."

"I read that, too," said Reese. "Did you know he started playing guitar when he was only five? He has such a great voice."

Jade sat down on the sofa beside Reese.

"I love his new album," said Jade. She leaned forward and rested her chin in her hands. Both girls watched the screen, staring at the singing guitarist.

I stared from one friend to the other in amazement. Were these the same two girls who had hated the sight of each other just two minutes ago?

As soon as the clip finished, Jade ran to her room. She returned waving her MP3 player. She quickly hooked it up to some speakers next to the TV.

With the music turned up loud, Reese and Jade began to dance. Both girls were grinning crazily.

I sat down onto the sofa. I didn't know the song, and I wasn't crazy about dancing. Staring at my friends, I opened a can and took a gulp of the fizzy drink. The two girls dancing around the room seemed to have forgotten all about me.

Finally, Jade and Reese stopped dancing and ran over to the coffee table. With the music still playing loudly, they attacked the food. As they scooped up dips with their crackers and slurped their drinks, Reese and Jade began making up for that afternoon's lost time.

"What other music do you like?" Reese wanted to know.

Jade began reeling off the names of the bands and artists in her music collection.

"I just downloaded Emma Short's new album," Reese said proudly.

Jade squealed. "I love her! Have you heard her new single, 'Life's Like That'? Hey! She's coming here on tour next month. She's playing at the arena. Why don't I see if I can get tickets, and we'll go?"

"Great," said Reese. "I could get Mum to bring me down for the night and meet you there."

I frowned. What in the world? Now they were suddenly going to a concert together? What about me? Was I going to be invited, too, or had they totally forgotten about me?

I wondered again how I could have been getting to know Reese ever since my move to Ridgeview and not have known she was such a music nut. I liked music, too. But after being the only one to keep the conversation alive all day, I suddenly found it impossible to get a word in. Every time I opened my mouth to speak, either Jade or Reese would start babbling on about every band that ever existed. Jade grabbed her MP3 player.

"Which would you rather listen to?" she asked Reese. "The Fireflies or Tom Taylor?"

"I thought we were watching *Glitter Girl*," I said grumpily.

"Oh," said Jade, sounding disappointed, but slightly guilty, as if she had suddenly remembered that I was in the room. "Did you want to?"

I abruptly rose from the couch. "Forget it," I snapped. "I'm going to bed." Then, looking at Reese, I added, "We have to get up early in the morning."

"Okay, see you," Reese said, without looking up. She was scrolling through the songs on Jade's MP3 player.

"Good night," said Jade, as I left the room.

I heard her but didn't answer.

I changed into my pajamas and scrambled inside one of the sleeping bags on the floor of Jade's room. I lay awake for a long time, listening to the muffled sound of the music and the other girls' voices.

Chapter Eleven

"Annie," a voice whispered close to my ear.

Sleepily, I opened one eye to see my mother's face. I could hear Jade snoring softly nearby. Reese rose from her sleeping bag and rubbed at her eyes.

"What time is it?" Reese quietly asked my mum.

"It's 6 a.m. We have to get going now if we're going to get you there in time for the first event." Mum glanced at the lump in

Jade's bed. "Try not to wake up Jade," she said quietly.

But Reese shook her head. "Jade's coming, too. She wants to watch."

I was scrambling to get dressed. As the substitute rider, I had to be dressed in my uniform and ready to ride, the same as the rest of the team. I looked up when I heard Reese. "When did you guys decide that?" I asked.

"Last night after you went to bed," Reese replied, then turned back to Mum. "We could drop her back here on the way home. If that's all right with you, of course."

I frowned angrily. Jade and Reese had made more plans without me.

Mum nodded. "I'll just check with her mum," she said and left the room. Before she'd closed the door, Reese was up and shaking Jade awake.

* * *

The drive to the riding school was shorter than the previous day's drive had been. That was lucky, as far as I was concerned. Thanks to Jade's slow start, we were running late.

Now, as I sat in the back of my parents' car with the other girls, I found myself left out again. Jade had brought along her MP3 player. She and Reese each had an earphone jammed into an ear. They were swaying to music that I couldn't hear. I just stared out the window.

After driving for about an hour, Dad turned the car onto a quiet, leafy street. We weren't the only arrivals. Behind us, turning onto the same street, was a small parade of 4×4s, all towing horse trailers.

I looked at the surroundings. Past huge, wrought-iron gates and large stone pillar entrances, we could see large, sprawling houses.

My father, who sold houses for his job, was impressed. "These places must be worth a fortune," he said, whistling as he looked at the big houses.

We were about to pass by a giant brick entrance. Just then, Reese suddenly tore the earphone from her ear and pointed. "That's the place," she said. "I remember it from last year."

Dad braked and turned into the driveway. Jade was still only listening to her music, but Reese was suddenly excited. She turned to me. "I hope Jefferson had a good night in the stable. He's not used to staying away from home."

I nodded. I had been wondering the same thing about Bobby.

A narrow driveway opened up to a large car park. Even though it was early, the car park was already crowded with cars and horse trailers.

A parking attendant waved each vehicle in, directing them to park in rows. Many horses, wearing blankets and travelling boots, were being unloaded and tied to the sides of the trailers.

To the left was a big stable block, where Dad found a place to park against the wall.

Jade made a face. "What stinks?" she asked. But we ignored her. Reese and I were looking for our horses and the rest of our team.

"There's Mum," Reese said. She pointed at her mum's 4×4. "Come on, Annie," she said. "Let's find our horses. Then we'll have to see Mr Snyder."

"We'll see you girls later," Mum promised. "We're off to find coffee." She and Dad wandered off.

Reese took charge, dragging me with her. Jade followed, the MP3 player still in her hand.

Jade had dressed in city sandals, a trendy lace-edged skirt, and a top that showed part of her tummy. Here, where everyone was dressed in riding club jodhpurs and uniform sweaters in their various colours, she looked totally out of place.

"Why is everyone in such a rush?" Jade wanted to know.

"It's the games day," said Reese, sounding impatient. "It's a big deal. Everyone is part of a team. Some people look forward to this for the whole year."

Jade shrugged and rolled her eyes at me. "It's a really big deal, huh?" she asked sarcastically, nudging me.

But I wasn't paying attention. Just like the only other competition I'd been to, which had been a one-day event, I quickly found myself getting excited.

Everyone looked so busy. I could hear the clop of horse's hooves across the car park, and the rush of water from a tap as someone filled a bucket. I felt again the sting of knowing that I was just a substitute, instead of playing a true part in the games as a team rider.

Inside the stable block, the Ridgeview horses had all been assigned stalls in the same row. We spotted Ripple first. She was tied to a post outside her stall, saddled and ready to go.

Jessica stood nearby. She was ready to ride, dressed in expensive-looking jodhpurs. Her matching green velvet gloves and helmet, the exact same shade as her green riding club sweater, were more suitable for a show than a games competition.

Even though I knew that, I had to admit that Jessica looked nice. My own jodhpurs and uniform were hand-me-downs from Reese, who was taller and had outgrown them.

The grey and red heads of Jefferson and Bobby suddenly poked over the top of the stable doors. Bobby nickered softly when he saw me.

Reese and I rushed over to pat our horses. Reese's mother, Mrs Moriarty, was unpacking tack from an oversized canvas bag. She was talking with Mrs Coulson, Jessica's mother.

Jessica and her mother glared at us. No one paid any attention to Jade.

"You're late," Mrs Moriarty said. "I was beginning to wonder what had happened to you." She pointed to a stall a few doors up. Matt was busy saddling up Bullet. Austin and Mr Snyder were there, too. I didn't see Natalie.

"Since you're finally here, you need to go talk to Mr Snyder," Mrs Moriarty ordered firmly. "I just hope you get time to properly warm up your horses."

But Mr Snyder was already heading towards

us, looking directly at me. "Thank goodness you made it," he said with relief. "I'm counting on you both to come through for the team."

I noticed Matt and Austin smirking behind Mr Snyder. I was confused. Was Mr Snyder including me? What was he talking about, counting on us both? Reese would be riding, of course. But as the substitute rider, there wasn't much I would be doing to help.

"I'll try to support them as best as I can, Mr Snyder," I said.

"That's good news. I'll let you saddle up then," said Mr Snyder.

It took a moment for Mr Snyder's words to sink in. A faint hope stirred slowly inside me. Could this mean . . . could he possibly be saying. . .

"Saddle up?" I questioned.

Matt began to laugh. "She doesn't get it,

Dad," he said.

"Nope," said Austin. "She definitely doesn't get it. You'd better tell her about my sister."

Mr Snyder nodded. "The Ryans called half an hour ago. Austin came with us last night, but his parents and Natalie decided to leave home early this morning. Unfortunately their car broke down just a few minutes outside of Ridgeview. There's a mechanic looking at it, but there's no way they'll make it here in time. It's too bad for Natalie, but good for you."

Mr Snyder paused a moment before adding, "So, kiddo, you're in."

"I'm in," I repeated stupidly.

Then I squeaked with pleasure, jumping up and down on the spot as I realized what his words meant. I was a part of the team – for real this time!

A couple of people were watching me

curiously, no doubt wondering what the fuss was about. I didn't care. I was in, and that was all that mattered.

Chapter Twelve

Gear check had seemed to take forever, but now the team was lined up outside the roped-off games arena, waiting for our turn to race. Four rows of bending poles had been set up, with drums at either end to signify the start line and the turning point.

I glanced across the field to where spectators lined the ropes. They were grouped together with others from their own club. Enormous banners with oversized letters spelled out club names. Some people had set up folding chairs and umbrellas to watch the day's events, while others stood around.

Austin and Mr Snyder had set up a spot near the start line. Austin carried a clipboard and pen. He was going to be the club scorer for the day. As each heat was run, he would mark down the results and keep track of the score for Ridgeview.

Behind them, Dad was talking with Mrs Snyder. Even from this distance, I could see Jade's bored expression as she stood with my mother. Mum caught my eye from over the top of a dozen heads and smiled.

I tried to smile back, but the anxious knot in my stomach seemed to have spread to my face. So I just nodded.

For the third time, I wiped sweaty hands across my jodhpurs. My whole body trembled with nerves. Looking around, I knew I wasn't the only one. Horses stamped and fidgeted.

Some of the riders on the other teams looked as if they wanted to change their minds and leave.

Reese, Matt, Bryce, and Laura sat quietly on their mounts. Jessica brushed imaginary bits of lint off her sweater. She caught my glance and scowled. She had been the only one who didn't seem pleased that I was now on the team.

"Don't worry," Matt said to me. He leaned forward in the saddle and scratched Bullet's ears. "Everybody gets nervous, but once the first race starts, everything will just happen. Remember – if you make a mistake, just fix it and keep going."

Mr Snyder had already explained the day's programme to us. There were 24 teams, one from each club. The teams had been put into groups, four in each.

Team placings from each race were turned into points that would be added up at the end of the day. The two teams with the highest points would go to the county finals.

Suddenly, we were being called. We would be riding in the very first heat!

The races were fast and furious. If any of the riders made a mistake, someone would lift a red flag and hold it up until that rider went back and fixed the error.

Spectators cheered from the sidelines. The Ridgeview team flew through the bending race, finishing second in the heat.

That first winding canter through the poles settled my nerves. Once I was racing, the other teams and the noise from the crowd all faded into the background.

Instead of worrying about anything else, I just concentrated. I focused on moving Bobby in and out and passing the baton without dropping it.

Unfortunately, the rope race caused our team major problems. Each team only needed four riders, so Jessica and I watched and cheered from the sidelines.

Things went well for Laura and Bryce. Laura raced through the line of bending poles carrying a length of rope to where Bryce was waiting at the other end.

Once she'd reached him, Bryce grasped the opposite end of the rope, and the two of them wove back through the poles together, never letting go of the rope. Once they'd crossed over the start line, Laura dropped her end of the rope and Reese took her spot.

Together, Bryce and Reese turned to race back through the bending poles to where Matt was waiting. Jefferson didn't like having another horse so close to him. He moved away, knocking over one of the poles and causing Reese to drop her end of the rope.

We all gasped in horror as Reese hurriedly dismounted to fix the pole, then vaulted back into the saddle. They made it to the end, and Bryce and Matt quickly changed spots.

By that time, however, the team trailed badly. Reese and Matt did their best to catch up, but couldn't make up enough ground. Ridgeview finished last.

Next came the stepping-stones race. Reese rode out first. She managed to keep a slight lead while leaping from her horse to step over the row of concrete blocks, then swinging back into the saddle and galloping around the drum and back again.

Jessica had some trouble remounting, losing time for the team. Luckily, Bryce managed to make it up again on his run. Laura kept the lead. It seemed to me that Laura's feet flew over the stones. Then she was back in the saddle and flying towards me.

Bobby knew what was expected of him. He took off cantering the moment Laura passed the line.

I heard nervous shouts as I got closer to the stepping stones. I knew right away that we were travelling too fast. I thought about my options.

I could try a mobile dismount. I had seen Matt do it often enough.

I knew, though, that a move like that was a huge risk. If it went wrong, I might fall flat on my face, lose time, and possibly make the team lose the race. But on the other hand, if it went right. . .

The stepping stones were in front of me. I had to make a decision – fast. We were only a couple of strides away. . .

I kept my hands firmly on the reins and swung my leg out of the saddle while still cantering. Bobby slowed. I hit the ground with both feet running, just in time to tiptoe across the stones.

After my spectacular dismount, I briefly considered whether I should try to vault on but decided it was too risky. I stopped Bobby to remount and then cantered on, around the drum and back to Matt, who yelled encouragement at my approach.

Once Matt began the final leg of the race, I felt like I could breathe again. I was having a great time, but I didn't want to make any mistakes that could cost points for the team. The whole team was yelling now. I joined in as I watched Matt and Bullet flash their way to the stones. Matt dismounted, crossed the stones, and vaulted back on to fly home. The other teams didn't stand a chance.

Matt and Bullet crossed the line. Our teammates screamed happily. It was only the third race. But for me and the rest of the Ridgeview team it was a huge victory after losing so badly in the rope race.

We left the arena with big grins. I slapped out high-fives to the others in turn. My palm made contact with Jessica's. We smiled. Today we were a team.

"Go Ridgeview!" Matt yelled.

The host riding club provided lunch. We were each given a drink, sandwiches, fruit, and a chocolate bar. The horses rested in their stalls, while Mr Snyder disappeared into the officials' tent.

Our team gathered folding chairs and sat under a tree to eat. The morning's activities had left us grubby and hot. Even Jessica had a dark smear of dirt across the knee of her jodhpurs. She was wiping at it with one hand while trying to hold on to her sandwich with the other.

Then my parents appeared with Jade. While the adults chatted, I introduced Jade to the others in the group. I noticed Jessica watching Jade with interest.

"So who won?" Jade asked in a bored tone.

We all stared at Jade in disbelief. I didn't even know what to say.

"It's not over yet," Reese told her. "Haven't you been paying attention?"

Jade flipped back her hair and rolled her eyes. "Well, it's not exactly the Olympics, is it?" she said.

"So why did you come, then?" Reese challenged.

"I really don't know," Jade shot back. "If I'd known you'd all be prancing around in the dust – and worse – I wouldn't have wasted my time."

Reese turned her back on Jade in disgust. I sighed. Obviously Reese and Jade's brief moment of togetherness was over.

I wondered why Jade was acting like such a brat. Back when we had shared everything, Jade had always said she loved horses as much as I did.

Jessica moved over next to Jade. "Not all horse riders like dirt and manure, you know," Jessica told Jade sweetly. "By the way, I love your skirt. Where did you get it?"

Jade seemed happy to have found someone to talk to. She and Jessica started talking about clothes and shopping. I felt another stab of jealousy. My best friend getting on well with Jessica, of all people.

Austin walked over. "You guys have scored points in two out of the three races, which puts us into third position," he told us.

"It's not a bad start," said Matt. "But we'll have to do better if we're to make it to County. We have to try and win all three races to be sure of a place."

"But no pressure, right, Matt?" Reese muttered.

I groaned. "That's impossible," I wailed. "The sack race is next. I'll fall over."

"No, you won't," said Laura. "Besides," she added, shooting an angry look at Matt, "we all make mistakes. And so do the other teams. Just do your best, Annie. That will be more than enough."

The sacks turned out to be bigger than the ones we had practiced with. I wasn't sure if that would be better or worse. Thankfully, my team wasn't racing yet.

I watched the other races. Lots of riders were having trouble running in the sacks, and there were plenty of falls. That made me feel a little less nervous. At least I wouldn't have the embarrassment of being the only person to fall over in front of everyone.

This time I was first to start. A sack had been laid out on the ground at the end of each team's lane. I cantered Bobby to the sack.

I dismounted and climbed into the sack while holding onto one of Bobby's reins. I could hear my team members yelling encouragement as I began to jump.

I concentrated on keeping my toes pushed firmly into the bag. The girl in the next lane fell and had trouble getting up. I tried to focus on the finish line. If I stayed focused, I might just be able to make it.

My jumps became faster as I slowly moved closer to the line. Reese sat on Jefferson, waiting to take the bag from me.

One jump closer, another . . . suddenly I was there, scrambling out of the sack and handing it to Reese, who cantered away the instant she grabbed it.

I did it! I relaxed. My job was done, at least for this race.

By the time Matt took his turn to climb inside the sack, Ridgeview had gained a small lead over the others in the race. He and Bullet took off at a gallop, then screamed to a halt at the end of the lane.

Matt had perfected his own amazing style of sack-jumping. He held the bag up as tight as he could and scooped along, dragging one foot forward and then the other. It looked crazy, and I had laughed the first time I saw him do it. But Matt's odd-looking sack shuffle was fast and worked, and by the time he was halfway back he had gained a good lead.

Then the unthinkable happened.

Bullet, trotting steadily along beside Matt, moved too close and stood on the corner of the sack. Everyone on our team gasped as Matt went down. The other teams closed in while Matt struggled to get back on his feet and get going again.

Matt hurried to make up ground and fell across the line to finish, but it wasn't fast enough. Before he could make it, another team pulled ahead and beat him. Matt looked pretty upset as we all waited back in the warm-up area for the next race.

"I lost the race," Matt announced sadly. "If we don't get to County, it's all my fault."

We all argued with Matt. It wasn't his fault. It was bad luck. He couldn't blame himself. All of us had made mistakes, after all. Making mistakes was part of the competition. But Matt's shoulders slumped. He stared down at his saddle.

I felt bad for him. I knew how badly Matt and his dad had wanted to make the county finals. Now, even if Ridgeview won both the five-flag and the bottle race, it might not be enough to get us in.

We won both our heats in the five-flag race and the bottle race. Matt rode his best ever, and the rest of us did, too. But it wasn't like the glorious moment after we had won the stepping-stone dash that morning. We felt terrible. We hadn't made it to County after all.

Jessica tried to make us feel better, but she just made everyone feel worse. "They're only games," she said. "It's not like we were beaten for Supreme Champion or something."

If I had held something in my hand, I might have thrown it at Jessica. We were disappointed for Matt's sake. Couldn't Jessica see that? Now he would be waiting a whole year for another chance at the county finals.

Back at the stalls, we dismounted, preparing to unsaddle. Then a crackling voice came over the loudspeaker. "Riders from Ridgeview Riding Club and Glenhope Riding Club, please return to the games area. I repeat, riders from Ridgeview Riding Club and Glenhope Riding Club, please return to the games area."

Puzzled, we looked around at each other.

"What's going on?" someone asked.

Leading our horses, all six riders trooped back to find out why we'd been called. Spectators were standing around. I picked up snatches of excited conversation as we passed through.

"Equal points. . ." said one person.

". . . decide the place. . ." someone else said.

Mr Snyder stood, waiting for us. Delighted, he passed on the news. "You tied for second place," he announced. "There'll be a race-off to see which team goes on to County."

Mr Snyder's words were met with a stunned silence. Then everybody began talking at once.

"Which race?" asked Bryce.

"We can beat Glenhope," Laura said.

"We don't have a choice," Matt said.

By the time the competing teams gathered for the race-off, the light was beginning to fade. Shadows darkened the games arena, and the air was much cooler.

The race-off event was going to be the bottle race. Silently, I thanked the organizers for not running the sack race again. I waited with the others, mounted on our horses outside the arena, while the race officials prepared the field.

My body was tight with tension. I could feel it filling my chest, swirling like fog. I knew the others felt it, too.

The teams were called to line up. A hush had fallen over the spectators. In the last moments before the start, the only sounds that could be heard were the jangle of bits in the horses' mouths. Someone's horse snorted. The riders were silent, focused – waiting.

The starter called, "Prepare to race." One second later the world went wild. The crowd was suddenly alive, cheering, screaming at their teams to go, go, GO!

Bryce took off, never taking his eyes from the bottle on the drum ahead of him. I was next. I watched Bryce's progress while trying to block out the roaring in my ears. Bobby pranced beneath me.

Bryce and his horse charged towards me. Bryce's outstretched arm held the bottle. He wasn't slowing. Bryce was taking a huge risk. I would have to snatch the bottle as he passed. In all the practice sessions, and even here today, no one had passed to me at such speed. The passing rider would always slow down. Could I grab the bottle without dropping it?

I held out my hand. My world narrowed until the only thing left in it was one small bottle. Then Bryce was there. My fingers closed around the bottle's neck.

I had it!

I kicked Bobby into action, but he was already halfway towards the drum. I slowed the horse and swung down to drop the bottle. Bryce might have taken a risk, but I wanted to be sure. It was important to get it right. If the bottle didn't stay upright, I would waste time going back to fix it.

Carefully, I dropped the bottle on the drum. It stayed. My attention went instantly to the next drum. I got closer to the bottle. A large shape flashed past in the next lane. Oh no! The rider from the other team was getting ahead.

I frowned. I wasn't sure what to do. If I slowed down now, I would waste more time. Then the other rider would gain an even bigger lead. If I took a chance and slipped up, my team would be in trouble.

Then suddenly the bottle was there. I had no time to slow down, so I leaned down as far as I could without falling out of the saddle and swept up the bottle. It slid down through my hands.

I was terrified as I felt the bottle sliding through my fingers. It had almost dropped when I clamped it hard against Bobby's shoulder. Bobby, feeling me press him in a strange place, tried to move away.

I heard a gasp from the spectators. I tipped sideways but managed to hold myself up and stay in the saddle. Holding the bottle against Bobby had given me time to adjust my grip. My grasp on the bottle was firm as I thundered back towards Jessica, who waited to take her turn.

The pass was clean. Thank goodness! I looked back to see Jessica and the other team's rider reach their drums at the same time.

"Go, Jessica!" I screamed. All of us cheered and hoped Jessica could take the lead.

The pair passed the line together. Laura, then Reese, rode perfectly but just couldn't manage to shake the other team. It was an even race.

By the time Matt snatched the bottle from

Reese for the final leg, my throat hurt from screaming. The crowd was screaming, too.

As Matt rode past, the first bottle landed on the drum.

I had been so impressed by Matt's skill at games, but I could hardly believe the sight of the Glenhope rider, another boy about Matt's age. He was not only keeping up with Matt, but he also seemed just as skilled as Matt was.

Both riders swooped on the final bottle, clutching it tightly as they made their turns around the drum. The other rider got ahead.

I stared, worried. Ridgeview was so close. How could we lose now?

The thing that happened next was something that would be talked about at riding club meetings across the county.

I heard a sudden roar from the spectators, and then saw the Ridgeview flag raised. Matt had dropped the bottle!

The Glenhope rider glanced across into Ridgeview's lane. His horse looked around, then tripped. I watched in disbelief as the other rider's bottle tumbled to the ground, too.

Incredible! Another flag came up.

Both riders were off their horses and grabbing at the bottles right away. But Matt had a secret weapon. While the Glenhope rider was still reaching for his stirrup to remount, Matt vaulted up and onto Bullet's back.

Matt and Bullet raced across the line. Ridgeview was headed to the county finals!

I knew I would never forget being a part of the Ridgeview team that day.

Mr Snyder ran around shaking everybody's hand and slapping shoulders. He lifted me up in a bear hug. "I knew you could do it, Annie! I just knew it," he shouted.

None of us could stop smiling. Parents milled around the team.

Mrs Moriarty hugged Reese. "We're going to the county finals," Reese's mum said. "We're going to win!"

"Sure, Mum," Reese answered, laughing.

Reese's eyes found mine over her mother's shoulder. "Told you," she mouthed. But she was grinning.

Jade had forgotten to be bored. "That was the most exciting race," Jade told me.

"Not so boring, huh?" I said, laughing.

Reese thanked my family and said goodbye to Jade. She was driving home with her mother and the horses. I noticed that she didn't mention going to the Emma Short concert with Jade.

My family dropped Jade off at her house on the way home. I got out of the car to say goodbye. "Thanks for coming to watch today," I told Jade.

"It was cool," said Jade. Then she added, "Well, actually, it was nothing like I imagined. I had no idea you could ride so well."

I smiled. "I'm not that good, really. Not like some of the other kids at the club. There's so much to learn. Riding has been a lot harder than I thought it would be. But I love it. Today was awesome."

"I don't think the whole horse scene is for me," said Jade. "You're just lucky you have me around to keep you socially acceptable."

We hugged each other. Then I got into the car. From the back seat, I waved until the car turned the corner and Jade was out of sight.

I yawned. I was so tired that I felt dizzy. I was glad that Jade and I were still friends. But a lot had changed since I moved to Ridgeview.

I relived the day in my head. I was still smiling as I fell asleep.

It was dark when I woke up. Our car pulled into the Hillgrove driveway. Mrs Moriarty was already parked in the driveway with the horse trailer. Using a torch and the car headlights to see, Reese was in the process of backing Bobby off the ramp. I took Bobby's rope from Reese's hand.

"The county finals are next month," said Reese. "Matt's already setting up practice days."

"Has he come back down to earth yet, do you think?" I asked.

"It was an amazing day, though, wasn't it?" Reese asked. "You were great. I couldn't believe it! You'll be vaulting next. Just wait."

I beamed at the compliment. "After seeing the way Matt's vaulting saved us in that last race, I really want to learn." I paused for a moment. "You know, I honestly thought you guys didn't want me on the team. I mean, I'm such a beginner, I don't really fit in with the rest of you, do I?"

Reese pushed playfully at my shoulder. "What are you talking about?" she asked, shaking her head. "Of course you fit in. And I'd hardly call you a beginner these days. You ride as well as any of us."

I stared at Reese, who added, "The only thing I was worried about was Matt trying to pressure you into riding. He's so crazy about the games. For all we knew, you might not have even wanted to ride with us today."

"What about Jessica?" I asked. "She didn't want me on the team, I'm sure of that."

Reese laughed. "Jessica doesn't want anybody near her if she thinks they might show her up," she told me, smiling. "Honestly, Annie, she's just annoyed because you ride as well as her, if not better."

I unlatched the gate and walked Bobby into his paddock. I stood with him for a moment. He leaned into me while I scratched his ears.

Dad's voice carried faintly across the night air. "Those kids were all pretty good out there today," he was saying. "I didn't know you could train horses to do all that stuff."

I chuckled to myself. What did he think we did at the riding club?

"At County, they can do even better and bring home the blue ribbon," Mrs Moriarty was saying.

Typical, I thought. Reese was right about Mrs Moriarty. She was pushy.

Mrs Moriarty was still talking to Dad. "Why don't you come to a rally?" Reese's mum asked. "We can always use more adult helpers. Annie's riding is really coming along, you know."

I stood quietly, trying to hear my father's next words. He had never shown any interest in the riding club.

"Well, she looked like she knew what she was doing out there today." He sounded pleased. "Maybe I should go take a look."

"Of course," said Mrs Moriarty, "a lot of the credit has to go to the horses. Bobby is a real gem. Annie had a lucky break when she found him."

"Hmm," said Dad. "I guess she did."

Was that my dad? I could hardly believe my ears.

I slipped the halter over Bobby's ears. Through the darkness, I watched his outline as he headed away, snatching bites of grass.

I sighed happily. Settling into my new life in Ridgeview was turning out better than I'd ever thought possible. Hillgrove was a nice place to live. I had a good job at Erica's stables, school was turning out okay, and I loved the riding club.

I took one last long look at the shadowy outline of my horse.

Bobby was the best of the best.

About the Author

When she was growing up, Bernadette Kelly desperately wanted her own horse. Although she rode other people's horses, she didn't get one of her own until she was an adult. Many years later, she is still obsessed with horses. Luckily, she lives in the country, where there is plenty of room for her four-legged friends. When she's not writing or working with her horses, Bernadette and her daughter compete in riding club competitions.

Horse Tips from Bernadette

- Horses can learn bad habits just as quickly as they can learn good ones. The rider is the person who teaches the horse, so make sure you teach him the right way. If you don't know what that is, then get someone who knows about horses to help you.

- Stay calm and keep your patience when around horses.

- Always ride with consideration for your horse.

- Learn everything you can about horses.

For more, visit Bernadette's website at
www.bernadettekelly.com.au/horses

ᴄ Glossary ᴐ

⊙ **baton** short stick passed from one person to another in a relay race

⊙ **canter** move at a speed between a gallop and a trot

⊙ **desensitize** make someone less scared of or shocked by something

⊙ **disqualified** prevented from taking part because a rule was broken

⊙ **dressage** riding and training a horse

⊙ **humiliation** embarrassment

⊙ **jodhpurs** trousers worn for riding

⊙ **obsessed** thinking about it all the time

⊙ **paddock** enclosed area where horses can graze or exercise

⊙ **spectator** someone who watches an event

⊙ **substitute** rider who will participate if someone else is unable to

⊙ **vault** leap

Advice from Annie

Dear Annie,

I have two best friends. I know, I'm lucky to have two. But the problem is, they don't get along at all! We can't ever hang out together because they fight the whole time. What can I do? I like both of them, and I wish they liked each other. Help!

Wondering in Winchester

Dear Wondering in Winchester,

That's a tricky one! You're right, you are lucky to have two best friends. But when they don't get along, it sometimes feels like you have no friends at all! I have a few ideas that might help.

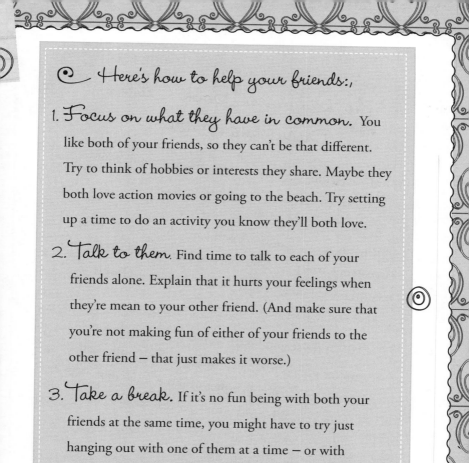

⊙ Here's how to help your friends:

1. **Focus on what they have in common.** You like both of your friends, so they can't be that different. Try to think of hobbies or interests they share. Maybe they both love action movies or going to the beach. Try setting up a time to do an activity you know they'll both love.

2. **Talk to them.** Find time to talk to each of your friends alone. Explain that it hurts your feelings when they're mean to your other friend. (And make sure that you're not making fun of either of your friends to the other friend — that just makes it worse.)

3. **Take a break.** If it's no fun being with both your friends at the same time, you might have to try just hanging out with one of them at a time — or with other friends. This doesn't mean giving up, but it does mean allowing yourself to have fun!

Good luck! You're a great friend — I hope your friends can be too!

Love,
♡ Annie

The Ridgeview Book Club Discussion Guide

Use these reading group questions when you and your friends discuss this book:

1. What is Jessica Coulson's problem? She seems to treat everyone badly. Do you know anyone like Jessica? Without naming names, discuss ways to deal with bullies like Jessica.

2. When Reese and Jade first meet, they don't seem to like each other. Then they get along really well. Annie isn't happy in either of those situations. Talk about this. Why isn't Annie pleased when her friends dislike or like each other? How would you feel in either of those situations?

3. Annie's relationship with her dad is complicated. Talk about it. What steps could she and her dad take to make their relationship better? What other problems do people your age have with their parents? What can be done to make a family better?

The Ridgeview Book Club
Journal Prompts

A journal is a private place to record thoughts and ideas.
Use these prompts to get started. If you like, share your
writing with your friends.

1. What are the benefits of being part of a team? Write
about being a member of a team. What is good about it?
What can be bad? What are some of your experiences of
being on a team?

2. Friendships are complicated. Write about a time that
two of your friends didn't get along. What happened?
How did you feel about it? How was the problem
resolved? What do you think you'll do about it if it
happens again?

3. It feels great to win. Write about winning. What did
you win? How did you feel? Who helped you win?
Did anyone or anything stand in your way?

RIDGEVIEW RIDING CLUB

Team Challenge

BERNADETTE KELLY

RIDGEVIEW RIDING CLUB

Heads or Tails?

BERNADETTE KELLY

RIDGEVIEW RIDING CLUB

Balancing Act

BERNADETTE KELLY

RIDGEVIEW RIDING CLUB

Making Waves

BERNADETTE KELLY

RIDGEVIEW RIDING CLUB

Taking a Break

BERNADETTE KELLY